William's Journal

by Ellen Doherty

illustrated by Mark Corcoran

William Ferguson was 10 years old when he left Ireland to move to America with his mother, father, and 6-year-old sister, Nelsey. This is the diary he kept of their journey.

April 4, 1910

Mum and Da gave me this journal to write in because they say we're going on a grand adventure, and I'll want to remember every minute of it. Mum, Da, Nelsey, and I are going to America!

America is a big place, and it's full of people and jobs. That's what Uncle John wrote to us. He's lived in New York City since before I was born.

To get to America, we're going to take a big ship. I've never been on a boat in my life! I hope I don't get seasick.

May 21, 1910

We're leaving for New York soon. We can only take a couple of things with us, so we must choose what's most important. Mum says she won't leave without the lace tablecloth Gran made. I'll take my tin whistle and this journal.

June 1, 1910

It's so strange. Our house is almost empty. We had to sell just about everything we had to buy the tickets.

Before I thought it would just be fun, and exciting, too. But now I'm thinking about how I won't see my friends and Gran anymore. I'm really going to miss them all.

June 4, 1910

Today is the day we leave for America. I hope I always remember what it was like to live here in Ireland. We had a cottage with a thatched roof and whitewashed walls. There's a big field out back that leads up to a forest. It's a brilliant place to play. There's a river, too, where Da and I went fishing.

June 10, 1910

I think this boat is bigger than our village! There are so many people—more than I've ever seen in my life.

We are traveling below deck. It's crowded and dirty down here. Mum says as long as we're together, we'll be fine.

This is my family on deck.

June 12, 1910

The air is so bad below deck that lots of people have been sick. Nelsey's been throwing up a lot. I feel bad for her. I took out my tin whistle a little while ago to play her favorite tune. It made her smile, so I played another. Pretty soon, a man started playing a fiddle, and people danced. It felt just like a party back home.

June 16, 1910

Last night there was a huge storm. The ship was pitching and rolling on huge waves. That's what the sailors told me, anyway. All I know is that I threw up a lot!

Soon we will be in New York!

It was a dark and Stormy night.

June 21, 1910

I saw her! I saw the Statue of Liberty before anyone else. Mum says I have eyes like a hawk. The statue stands on her very own island in New York Harbor. And she's huge!

We're waiting to go to Ellis Island, where they look you over before they let you into America.

Mum has us in our best clothes, so we will make a good impression when we arrive in New York.

I can see New York City from here. There are lots of buildings. Somewhere over there is where I'm going to live!

June 23, 1910

Here's what happened on Ellis Island. We got off the boat and went into a big building. First thing we did was leave our luggage in the luggage room. Mum didn't want to, but Da convinced her it would be fine because the people who worked there would watch our belongings.

Next, we went up a big staircase to the second floor. There were a lot of people, so we had to wait a long time. Some doctors and nurses looked at our eyes and ears to make sure we're healthy. We are!

Other people asked what we were going to do in America. Da said we're going to live with Uncle John, and that he would have a job at a factory. Next thing I knew, we were allowed to go. A lady said, "Welcome to America!"

While we were waiting for the ferry boat to take us to New York, a clerk asked if he could take a photograph of us. Mum said yes, and wasn't it a good thing we were wearing our best clothes?

There was a huge crowd waiting when we got to New York. I saw a man who looked just like Da. I knew it had to be Uncle John. Da spotted Uncle John, and the two of them starting whooping and hollering! They hadn't seen each other in 15 years.

Next to Uncle John was a boy who looked like he was my age. This had to be my cousin Pat. We got off to a grand start. He helped us carry our things.

June 24, 1910

Our new home is an apartment in a building that's about four stories tall. It's small, but I think it's going to be great.

Da and Uncle John haven't stopped talking. Mum is helping Aunt Angela make dinner. Nelsey's playing with Pat's three little sisters. That's a lot of girls. Pat says he's happy to have another man around the house.

Got to go for now. Pat says we have just enough time before dinner to play a game of stickball with his friends. I think I'm going to like it here!